poems by
VERLIE HUTCHENS

trees by
JING JING TSONG

BEACH LANE BOOKS
New York   London   Toronto
Sydney   New Delhi

BEACH LANE BOOKS · An imprint of Simon & Schuster
Children's Publishing Division · 1230 Avenue of the Americas,
New York, New York 10020 · Text copyright © 2019 by Verlie
Hutchens · Illustrations copyright © 2019 by Jing Jing Tsong
· All rights reserved, including the right of reproduction
in whole or in part in any form. · BEACH LANE BOOKS is
a trademark of Simon & Schuster, Inc. · For information
about special discounts for bulk purchases, please contact
Simon & Schuster Special Sales at 1-866-506-1949 or
business@simonandschuster.com. · The Simon & Schuster
Speakers Bureau can bring authors to your live event. For
more information or to book an event, contact the Simon
& Schuster Speakers Bureau at 1-866-248-3049 or visit
our website at www.simonspeakers.com. · Book design by
Lauren Rille. · The text for this book was set in Filosofianow. ·
The illustrations were rendered as a digital collage of block
print and hand painted elements. · Manufactured in China
· 1218 SCP · First Edition · 10 9 8 7 6 5 4 3 2 1
· Library of Congress Cataloging-in-Publication Data ·
Names: Hutchens, Verlie, author. | Tsong, Jing Jing,
llustrator. · Title: Trees / Verlie Hutchens ; illustrated by
Jing Jing Tsong. · Description: First edition. | New York :
Beach Lane Books, 2019. · Identifiers: LCCN 2018016833
| ISBN 9781481447072 (hardcover : alk. paper)
| ISBN 9781481447089 (eBook) · Subjects:
LCSH: Trees—Juvenile poetry. | Children's
poetry, American. · Classification:
LCC PS3608.U8585 A6 2019 |
DDC 811/.6—dc23 LC record
available at https://lccn
.loc.gov/2018016833

Thank you to Rachel,
my adventurous mom, who taught
me to love the great outdoors
—V. H.

For my dear husband, M. A.,
and the trees we have climbed
—J. J. T.

Each tree offers
a story
a clue
a dance
that makes it
its very own
self.

Maple sings to the heavens.
Reaching out,
she offers her precious sap
to celebrate the return of the light,
and sweeten the last days of winter.

Aspen, tall and graceful,
dances on her tippy toes.
Her golden leaves like castanets
shimmer in the breeze.

Oak stands strong,
rooted deeply in the earth,
his mighty branches held out
just so—
palms up,
to receive the joy of birds.

Silly Palm,
plain and skinny,
doesn't have one single branch.
She saves all her leaves
for her most amazing
hat.

Shy Pussy Willow
takes center stage
one week in spring
when kitten velvet buds
adorn her modest twigs.

Apple Tree,
wise and gnarled,
bends low,
his branches weighed down
with round red fruit
and age.

Little Red Bud plays hide-and-seek
in bare-branched woods
until pink-purple giggles
burst forth
and give her hiding place
away.

Spruce,
in blue porcupine armor,
aims for the sky.
Like an arrow,
his heart soars.

Dogwood bows beside the walk,
welcoming the guests.
He offers treats on silver trays—
canapés of sunshine
and pollen.

Sycamore, the fashion queen,
wears a jigsaw-puzzle gown
and big flashy leaves.
Fuzzy round baubles
dangle from her ears.

White Pine, unruly uncle—
large and messy,
shirttails flying,
buttons akilter,
shaggy hair unkempt.
He laughs too loud.

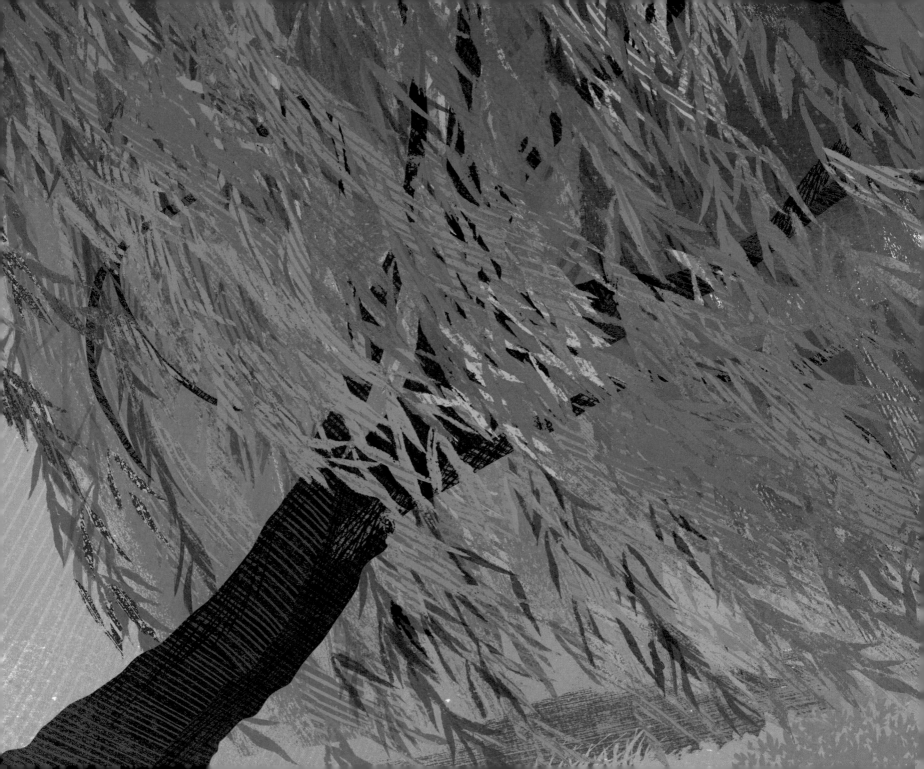

Willow dances
in her narrow kimono
with elegant sweeping sleeves
wafting
in gentle wind.

Birch,
when other trees
wear leafless black,
struts in
royal ermine robes.

Sequoia holds memories
for the Tribe of Trees,
telling tales from another age,
before the time
of saws.

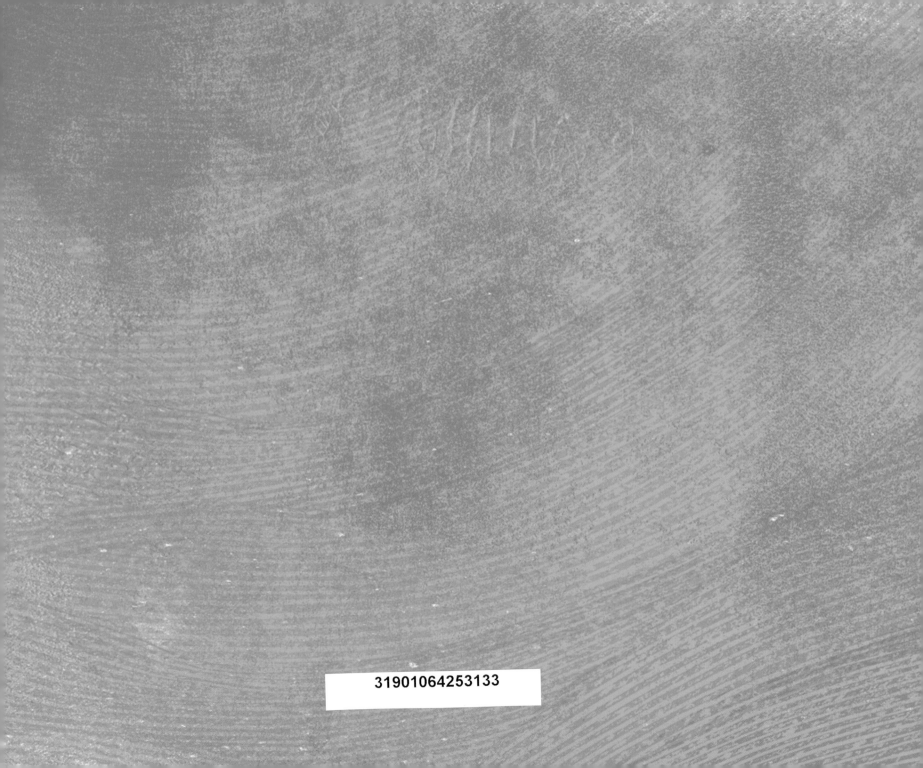